BENCHMARK BIOGRAPHIES

Jazz Is the Word
WYNTON MARSALIS

by Margaret Gay Malone

BENCHMARK BOOKS

MARSHALL CAVENDISH
NEW YORK

My thanks to the following people who were helpful in making this book a reality: my daughter, Michele, and friend Patricia Campbell Horton, for their much appreciated editorial comments; and Karin Barnaby, MaryAnne Cerny, Pam Levin, Dean Miller, Mark Morganelli, Terry Morganelli, Nancy Nicholson, Kathryn Satriani, and David Soto, who each helped me in a special way.

Special thanks to Renee Swanson and to my editor, Joyce Stanton.

And, of course, thanks to that incredible musician and gracious man, Wynton Marsalis.

Benchmark Books
Marshall Cavendish Corporation
99 White Plains Road, Tarrytown, New York 10591-9001

Library of Congress Cataloging-in-Publication Data
Malone, Margaret Gay.
Jazz is the word : Wynton Marsalis / Margaret Gay Malone.
p.   cm. — (Benchmark biographies)
Includes bibliographical references (p.   ) and index.
Summary: Discusses the life and musical career of the African American trumpet player known for his performances of popular jazz and classical music.
ISBN 0-7614-0519-4 (lib. bdg.)
1. Marsalis, Wynton, 1961–   —Juvenile literature. 2. Trumpet players—United States—Biography—Juvenile literature. [1. Marsalis, Wynton, 1961–   . 2. Trumpet players.]
I. Title. II. Title: Wynton Marsalis. III. Series.
ML3930.M327M35   1998   788.9'2'092   [B]—DC21   96-40410   CIP   AC   MN

Photo research by Margaret Gay Malone

Photo Credits
Front cover, back cover and pages 6, 8, 12, 21, 25, 28, 35 (top and bottom), 38: AP/Wide World Photos; pages 11, 15, 16 (left), 18, 22, 33, 39, 42: copyright Frank Stewart; page 16: courtesy of the Marsalis family; pages 31, 41: AP/LaserPhoto.

Printed in Hong Kong

1   3   5   6   4   2

To Lauren, Ryan, Robin, and Stacy,
the young people in my life,
with love

CONTENTS

Wynton gives the band the beat during a rehearsal for Jazz at Lincoln Center in New York City.

WYNTON LEARNS ABOUT SERIOUS FUN

The horns are lifted. The drumsticks are ready. Waiting. Then, *Unh, unh. Unh, unh, unh.* Wynton Marsalis gives his band the beat. They start to play. Hear the low *plum, plum, plum* of the bass, the *husha, husha* of the brushes as they skate along the drums. The trumpet's sweet heat fills the room.

Jazz.

And Wynton Marsalis, the most famous jazz trumpeter in the world today, is doing what he has done since he was six: making music.

He loves to bring music to people, especially kids. When his band tours the country, he often visits schools.

Today he is in a barn at Tanglewood, a famous music center in Massachusetts. Believing that good clothes can make you feel good about yourself, he is dressed in a colorful print vest. He is teaching about music, making a tape for kids and families to watch. It is one of a series of tapes about jazz and classical

During a lesson at the Tanglewood music center, Wynton shows children that music can be serious fun.

music. He is famous for playing both types of music. It is unusual to be good at both.

He stands on a low stage talking about the structure of jazz. Kids sit all around him. Some sit in the rafters above him, swinging their legs as he speaks to them. He bounces a basketball and tosses it to a boy sitting nearby. The boy is surprised. That's what Wynton wants because he's describing syncopation, a musical beat that surprises the listener. He talks about "call and response," when one musical instrument "answers" another during a song. To show it, he and his band play the call, and the kids are to respond at a certain point. They call out, smile, get into the spirit of the music. They are involved.

He does a little march. With his voice, he imitates musical instruments. Sometimes he jokes. Most of the time he is serious because he's talking about music.

To Wynton, music is serious fun. "Participate," he tells the kids, "and you'll understand the fun of being serious."

BETTER THAN A VACATION

That's why he never takes a vacation. He's always working with his music or touring the world. From city to city, by bus or plane, he travels with his trumpet and his band. A vacation would take him away from music and audiences—kids and grown-ups. And he loves them too much. Wynton never leaves a place where he has performed until he has given his autograph to everyone who wants it or has posed for pictures with his fans.

BACKSTAGE WITH KIDS

Wynton tells kids who play the trumpet to bring their horns to his concerts. After one concert, five boys and a girl, all elementary-school age, wait backstage. The first boy holds his trumpet under his arm and smiles shyly. Wynton walks over and shakes the boy's hand.

"I'm Wynton. What's your name?"

"Johnny," the boy says softly, looking up at his hero.

"What are you going to play?" Wynton asks.

"I don't know," Johnny says. He has looked forward to this night. He wants to play, but suddenly he is nervous.

Wynton smiles and admires Johnny's horn. Soon they are talking. Johnny gets up his courage and plays. Wynton tells him what he likes about his playing, and tells him how to improve. "Buzz your lips this way," he says as he shows Johnny. "I'll hold up the trumpet so you know how it should feel."

Wynton holds the horn while Johnny blows into it. "Good," Wynton says. "Now practice that in front of the mirror every day."

Encouraged, Johnny promises to practice harder. He walks away smiling. Wynton gives the same kind of boost to each of the kids who play for him. One by one, he makes them all glad they play music. That's what Wynton does.

JAZZ GOES TO SCHOOL

Sometimes high school bands come to hear Wynton Marsalis perform. Any school band member who loves to play the trumpet will be invited to play a song

Backstage after a performance, a young trumpeter gets a lesson from Wynton.

"B-r-r-r-a-t!" Wynton makes his trumpet sound like an elephant, to the amusement of a group of elementary-school children.

with Wynton's band. Wynton loves that as much as the young trumpeter does.

Wynton enjoys going to high schools and colleges, too. He plays with each school band and talks with the kids. They discuss many things, including the importance of getting an education. Most often they talk about music. Wynton is happy when kids ask him how they can improve their playing.

Sometimes he will disagree with a student. A high school boy likes rap music. Wynton does not. They argue. Finally the boy gives up. Wynton has not changed the boy's mind, but he has given him something to think about.

If he has a chance, Wynton likes to play basketball with students in the school gym. Even though he grew up in a family where everyone made music, he always loved basketball. His father, Ellis Marsalis, played jazz piano. His mother, Dolores, was a jazz singer. His older brother, Branford, could play clarinet and piano by the time he was seven. Though Wynton loved music, he preferred to be on the basketball court, dribbling that ball, shooting for the hoop, making a basket. For a while it was all he thought about. But when he was twelve, someone made him decide to be the very best trumpet player he could.

It was someone he had never met.

MUSIC SLAM-DUNKS
BASKETBALL

Wynton grew up in the little town of Kenner, Louisiana, where he was born in 1961. Although it would be twelve years before the music of Clifford Brown would make him take the trumpet seriously, Wynton heard music all his life. He lived near the city of New Orleans, the home of jazz. There, in the daytime, you can hear a banjo player strumming on a street corner. You can hear the beat of the jazz bands as they march along outdoors—for parades, for fun, even for funerals. At night the sounds of jazz float from the clubs onto the street.

Young Wynton loved the music in New Orleans. But even in the quiet town of Kenner, plenty of music could be heard coming from the Marsalis house. There was Wynton's father, Ellis, on the piano; his brother Branford on the piano and clarinet. As soon as he was able, little Wynton loved to sit at the piano and make the keys go *plink, plink.*

Wynton and his father, Ellis, still enjoy playing a song together.

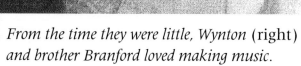

From the time they were little, Wynton (right) and brother Branford loved making music.

A grown-up Branford (left) listens while Wynton solos.

Before long Wynton was trying to play an old trumpet his father had. Ellis saw how much his son liked it. Luckily, he was working with famous trumpeter Al Hirt. He asked Mr. Hirt for money to buy six-year-old Wynton a trumpet. Mr. Hirt did better: He gave Wynton one of his.

Wynton felt like a grown-up musician playing the trumpet while his father played the piano. Wynton would play with Branford, who had begun to play the saxophone. Later their younger brother, Delfeayo, started studying the trombone. On holidays they played together, and the house sang to the sounds of the musical Marsalises.

THE BEST FEELING IN THE WORLD

At the Xavier Junior School of Music, where Wynton studied, the teachers expected their students to practice. Wynton was a very talented trumpet player, but he didn't practice as much as he should have.

"I'm going out now, Mama." Twelve-year-old Wynton stood at the door, a basketball under his arm.

"Did you finish your homework and your trumpet practice?" asked his mother.

"Most of it, Mom. I'll do the rest later." Wynton knew he had to finish his homework. In the Marsalis family, school was as important as music.

In a flash Wynton was out the door, dribbling the ball as he ran to the basketball court.

Basketball! He loved everything about it. To fly down a court; to leap for a

Wynton (right) *still enjoys a good game of basketball.*

basket, airborne like the ball. And when the ball popped off the rim and sank into the net with a *whoosh*, it was the best feeling in the world. At twelve Wynton liked the trumpet, but he *lived* for basketball.

BETTER THAN BASKETBALL

A recording by a trumpeter he had never met changed all that. When the Marsalises weren't making their own music, they were listening to other good musicians. Wynton was listening to a recording one night when he heard Clifford Brown on the trumpet. Brown made the trumpet sound warm, like a soft voice filled with emotion. It was the best trumpet playing he had ever heard. *Maybe I could play like that someday,* Wynton thought. He really wanted to be the best. Just like Clifford Brown.

Then Wynton remembered what his father had told him: if you want to be good, you have to do lots of "shedding." Musicians would often go to a woodshed to practice. The word *shedding* came to mean practicing. So Wynton began what he calls "serious shedding." In a book he wrote, *Sweet Swing Blues on the Road*, he says that for seven years he never missed a day of practice. And after that time, he still practiced nearly every day.

Practice began to pay off. At Benjamin Franklin High School, which he attended, everyone knew Wynton was a good trumpet player. But so was another classmate. They started a friendly competition. Who would play better? Wynton made up his mind it would be he. The rivalry made Wynton practice even harder.

CLASSICAL AND JAZZ

Wynton studied trumpet with John Longo, who played both classical music and jazz. Classical music flowered in Europe in the 1700s. Chamber music, opera, and symphony are some examples of classical music. It is more complex than popular or folk music. Jazz is genuine American music. It was first played by black musicians at the start of the 1900s. It is also complex. The rhythms are strong. Improvisation—making up a new version of the music as the musician is playing—is part of jazz. So are solos.

Although classical and jazz are each difficult to play, it is unusual to play both. Wynton loves both kinds of music, but he prefers jazz. He still keeps in touch with Longo, the man who showed him both worlds.

When he wasn't practicing, young Wynton listened to recordings of America's greatest trumpet players. Each one had a different style and Wynton knew them all. He liked Louis Armstrong, who, Wynton says, could do "whatever he wanted" with a trumpet. He liked Freddie Keppard because "he could make a horn laugh." And King Oliver, who "could make the trumpet sound like a chicken, cat, dog, elephant, or a woman sighin'."

Wynton played and listened, played and listened. Sometimes that meant he had to turn down a game of ball with his friends, but Wynton had made a choice—music came first—and he was never sorry.

A BAND OF HIS OWN

The better Wynton got on the trumpet,

Wynton likes his music and his clothes jazzy.

Wynton takes a turn at the keyboard while high school students listen and learn.

the more fun it was to make music. He and Branford played together often—classical duets by Mozart and Handel, and lots of jazz.

The brothers had just finished jamming one night. They smiled as they remembered the sound—the mellow call of the saxophone, the trumpet's sassy answer. They felt proud because they sounded good together. It was then that they decided to start a band of their own.

A drummer they knew joined them. Soon they added electric guitar and keyboard players. There were ten musicians in all. The Creators, as they named the group, played mostly rock music at high school dances, weddings, and talent shows.

It was not new for Wynton to play for a crowd. For years he had played in school bands. But he liked the idea of his own band. At fourteen he was at the start of a brilliant career, and one event helped launch it.

"SERIOUS SHEDDING" LEADS TO WINNING

"Wynton, the state is having a music competition. Any young person can enter. Would you like to?" His teacher stood there, smiling.

"Sounds good to me," said Wynton. The more he thought about it, the more excited he became. The winner would solo with the New Orleans Symphony.

Wynton imagined how it would be. The stage filled with professional musicians. His parents sitting in the front row, proud. He'd walk on stage, maybe play Haydn's trumpet concerto. Solo.

Solo? Wynton thought. *I'd better do some more serious shedding!*

Hundreds of kids from all over Louisiana entered the competition. Like the other young people, Wynton had to perform in front of a group of judges. They were musicians and music teachers, who graded the young performers. How difficult was the music? How well did the player know the piece? How good was his or her technique? These were the

Wynton credits his success to years of "shedding"—intense practice.

kinds of things the judges looked for.

Wynton played Haydn for them. After he finished, he looked at the judges' faces. He thought they might say something, but they didn't reveal how they felt. Wynton thought he had done a good job, but all he could do now was wait.

The news finally came: Wynton had won! Of all the young musicians in Louisiana, the judges had selected him.

THE BIG DAY

"Hurry up, Wynton. It's time to go," his mother said. Wynton took one last look in the mirror to straighten his tie. He wore his good suit. It was pressed, crisp. Looking good helped give him confidence. Today was a big day. He was going to perform with the New Orleans Symphony.

Wynton was excited as he walked onstage, the audience hushed, the orchestra waiting. He was nervous, too. Now he was glad for all the hours he had spent practicing.

The orchestra began to play. At a signal from the conductor, Wynton lifted his trumpet. With the first rich sounds, he began to relax. Everything felt right. He knew the trumpet was to be his life.

CLASSICAL OR JAZZ?—OR BOTH?

Wynton continued to practice every chance he got. He played with professional musicians—the New Orleans Civic Orchestra, the New Orleans Brass Quintet, and again with the New Orleans Symphony. He remembers that a famous trumpeter, Clark Terry, came to hear him play with the New Orleans

Symphony. Terry also sent Wynton a postcard while he was touring in Europe with his band. That was something, Wynton says, that he will never forget. Playing with professionals and being encouraged by them helped Wynton continue to follow his dream.

While he performed classical music with big orchestras, Wynton still wanted to play jazz more than anything else. He liked playing at Tyler's Beer Gardens, a restaurant in New Orleans, because the patrons loved to hear his trumpet swing.

When Wynton was seventeen, he and Branford played many musical engagements, or gigs, together. No matter how late they got home, their mother would have dinner waiting for her hardworking, hungry sons. They'd go to the room they shared and talk and talk, about their music and their plans.

Branford liked to hear music when he went to sleep, but Wynton needed quiet. After Branford fell asleep, his stereo silent, Wynton would lie awake in the dark, dreaming of the future.

SEVENTEEN AND TALENTED

"You have to be eighteen to audition for the Tanglewood music center," the men in charge told Wynton. But after the judges heard him play, they decided to set aside the age requirement. Not only did he study and play classical music with older musicians, but at the end of his studies, Wynton was given an award.

He was named Outstanding Brass Player. The other musicians marveled at his talent on the trumpet. One minute he played classical music perfectly; the

During a trumpet master class at Temple University, Wynton gives a student advice about his playing.

next minute, toe-tapping jazz.

Wynton wishes there were a place like Tanglewood where young people could study jazz. "I had to figure out how to play jazz myself," Wynton says. He learned by listening and by playing with many jazz greats.

After Tanglewood, when Wynton was still seventeen, he performed several times with Lionel Hampton, the great vibraphone player, and his band.

He still kept up his schoolwork and was a National Merit Scholarship finalist. Based on his test scores, he was one of the top high school students in the country. He could have gone to many fine colleges or universities. He chose the Juilliard School in New York City. Juilliard is a school for people who want to become performing artists and earn a college degree. Juilliard takes only the best students. Wynton stayed there for two years, but he was disappointed in the school. The teachers concentrated on classical music. He believed they didn't take jazz seriously.

TOURING WITH BLAKEY

Luckily he had a chance to play in a club with Art Blakey and his band, the Jazz Messengers. Wynton liked everything about Blakey—the man, his band, his style. Wynton believed he could learn more from Blakey than he could from Juilliard.

When Blakey asked him to tour with the band, Wynton was thrilled. Soon Blakey made him the band's musical director. Wynton was only nineteen. That's when he started to see newspaper articles praising his performances. He was beginning to be known around the country.

The next year he played with pianist Herbie Hancock's VSOP Quartet and began making recordings, including *Fathers and Sons*, with Ellis and Branford.

At age twenty Wynton had already accomplished a great deal. But there was much more to come.

WYNTON AROUND
THE WORLD

ynton started his own band and began to record both classical and jazz albums. His first album as a bandleader, called *Wynton Marsalis*, sold thousands of copies. It was named Best Jazz Album of the Year in the 1982 *Down Beat* reader poll. *Down Beat* magazine, which is all about musicians, named Wynton Best Trumpeter and Musician of the Year. He won over trumpeters Miles Davis and Dizzy Gillespie, who were older and more famous.

The mayor of New Orleans declared a Wynton Marsalis Day to honor him.

That was not all. The music industry's highest award, called the Grammy, is given at a ceremony much like that for the Academy Awards for films. In 1984 Wynton won not one but two Grammys, for best solo jazz performance, and for best classical performance. He became the first artist ever to receive awards for both classical and jazz music in the same year.

This antique phonograph was a gift from CBS Records for Wynton's dedication to education and music.

The more honors he received, the busier his days became. Wynton had more and more concert dates across the country, and more and more recording sessions. It seemed that everyone wanted to hear Wynton play the trumpet.

In the same year that he won the Grammys, he had a big disappointment. Half of his band left to play rock music.

Wynton wondered if young people were still interested in playing serious jazz. Then piano player Marcus Roberts joined the band. Wynton calls him The J Master because he is one of the finest jazz piano players in the world. Wynton let other fine musicians know he was rebuilding his band. With luck and his reputation for playing the best jazz, the best musicians came to him. Wynton says Roberts helped him build a band that was really serious about music. Roberts stayed with the group for six years. He still plays with them now and then.

LIFE ON THE ROAD

For years Wynton spent about nine months of the year on the road. He toured with his band—two saxophone players and men on trombone, bass, drums, and piano. The soundman is also an important part of the band. During performances he sits in front of an electronic soundboard, making sure that the sound has the right volume and quality. Wynton says the soundman is as much a part of the band as the performers.

The band traveled the country by plane, train, bus, and limousine. Because they spent so much of the time together

On their roomy touring bus, band members have a chance to relax and catch up on reading.

on the road, they shared a great deal besides their music. The bus they traveled in was just for the band. It was roomy, with tables, chairs, and some beds. The men could read, watch videos, talk, or catch up on their sleep.

Their favorite videos were of other musicians performing. If a musician was playing very well, the band stopped the tape, reran it—sometimes many times—and talked about the performance. They never stopped learning from other musicians.

Life on the road is not easy. Sometimes they would get to bed at 4:00 A.M. and have to get up at 5:30 a.m.! Wynton and the band members ironed their wrinkled clothes on tables in hotel rooms. They ate in "greasy spoons" when there were no good restaurants nearby. Sometimes

the band would arrive at an airport three hours early for a flight. Worse, they might get there just after the plane took off. Sharing difficult times made Wynton and his band members close friends.

GOOD TIMES AROUND THE WORLD

Fun followed the band, too, across America and in other countries, including England, France, Italy, Mexico, and Japan. Wynton and the men have many memories of good friends and good times in cities around the world. They ate raw fish and tofu in Chiba, Japan; finished every last barbecued chicken wing at a party in Winston-Salem, North Carolina; danced till early morning in Rochester, New York. They played the blues and ate dinner in a vineyard in Marciac, France. In cities across the United States they

Tenor Placido Domingo and Wynton play a concert in Brazil to help the environment.

Hot, foot-stompin' jazz at the JVC Jazz Festival at Lincoln Center. Wycliffe Gordon on trombone, Wynton on trumpet, and Wes Anderson on saxophone.

played encores in the street. The audience marched outdoors with them, New Orleans–style, stepping to a bouncy beat.

Wynton says one of the best parts of touring is meeting the people. "You get a feeling for them," he says. Even better, he says, is playing—just playing.

JAZZ COMES TO LINCOLN CENTER

Wynton has always believed in the importance of jazz. Lincoln Center in New York City is one of the best centers for music in the world. It used to be devoted to classical music—concerts, opera, and ballet. Wynton knew jazz belonged there, too.

In 1987 he brought jazz to Lincoln Center. He is the cofounder and artistic director of Jazz at Lincoln Center, which brings jazz performances to adults and special jazz performances to children. Jazz for Young People gives kids the opportunity to hear jazz and have Wynton explain the music. At a Saturday afternoon concert, Wynton can be seen wearing a snazzy vest, his trumpet in his hand, walking among the young people in the audience. He is doing one of his favorite things: bringing jazz and children together.

GRAMMYS AND KEYS TO THE CITY

Wynton's life is a whirlwind. New opportunities open up every day. He composes more now than ever before and tours less often. He is always getting ideas for a musical composition—anywhere, anytime. It could be late at night after a full evening of trumpet playing or just as he's opening his eyes in the morning. It could be in his New York City apartment, at the piano, at his desk, or in his bed. Or music could come to him while he is in the touring bus or at a hotel. He always takes time to write down the music that he hears in his mind. It is tiring work, but Wynton loves it.

PERFORMING, COMPOSING, AND MORE

Some of Wynton's projects in 1996 included composing music for dance. Music he wrote for the Alvin Ailey American Dance Theater had its premiere at Lincoln Center that year. He has also composed music for the Twyla Tharp Dancers and the New York City Ballet. Seeing beautiful dance movements

At home in his New York apartment, Wynton plays one of his compositions for ballet.

or hearing poetic lyrics have inspired Wynton to write music. Sometimes he carefully composes music to match the feeling of the dance or the words. Other times, just for fun, he will make up a melody on the spot.

Wynton still records classical music. In 1996 he recorded an album of the Brandenburg Concerto no. 2 in F Major and other pieces. He plays classical "to make sure I haven't been wasting time," he says in his book. He has not. His years on the trumpet keep improving his playing, whether it is classical or jazz.

In the first half of the 1990s, he recorded nine jazz albums, eight of them live at the Village Vanguard, a club in New York City. He likes recording live because someone listening to the album can hear the performers speak, hear the audience and their applause, and get a feeling of being there.

The Twyla Tharp dancers rehearse as Wynton conducts music he composed for the dance troupe.

Wynton also began writing long musical pieces in the early 1990s. In 1992 he wrote *Citi Movement*, music that expresses the energy of New York City. The listener can almost hear the sounds of traffic in this piece written for ballet. In 1994 he wrote *Blood on the Fields*, a musical piece about slavery.

Both *Blood on the Fields* and *Citi Movement* show the influence of Duke Ellington, a famous jazz pianist and composer. Wynton believes that Ellington was one of the finest jazz artists ever. Like Ellington's longer works, Wynton's longer pieces are similar to classical music. Wynton says people think of classical and jazz as separate, but they are really related.

Nineteen-ninety-six was a busy year for Wynton. He played at the closing ceremony of the 1996 Olympics. He worked on a twenty-six-hour radio series, *Making the Music*. He began writing the musical scores for two films, *Midnight Falls on Manhattan* and *Rosewood*. And he started work on a piece just for children. Called *Suite for Human Nature*, it combines theater, dance and music.

HONORS, HONORS, HONORS

Wynton has received many honors, from as far away as England, France, and Holland. Here in the United States, *Time* magazine named him one of the twenty-five most influential people in the country in 1996. A year later, he received the Pulitzer Prize for Music for *Blood on the Fields*. Wynton is the first person ever to receive a Pulitzer Prize for jazz. His collection of Grammy Awards has grown to eight.

Perhaps he is most proud of his keys to

*Wynton and fellow musicians Dr. John (left) and Jon Hendricks announce Grammy nominations
at the Hard Rock Café in New York City.*

Simeon (left) *and young Wynton with their father at a rehearsal.*

gig: a musical engagement, or job, for a period of time.

Handel, George Frideric: classical composer born in the 1600s. His most famous piece is the *Messiah*.

Haydn, Franz Joseph: classical composer who wrote his only concerto for trumpet in 1796.

improvisation: a musician's act of making up a new version of the music as he or she is playing or singing.

jazz: American form of complex music that originated with black musicians in the South around the start of the 1900s.

lyrics: words to a song.

Mozart, Leopold: the composer and violinist who lived from 1719 to 1787 and wrote symphonies, concertos, and sacred music. He is the father of the famous Wolfgang Amadeus Mozart.

solo: music played or sung by a single musician, often as part of an orchestra or band piece.

rhythm: the regular beat of the music.

syncopation: rhythm that accents a beat that is normally not accented.

tofu: bean curd, a food popular in Japan and China.

vineyard: area where grapes are grown.

Index

Page numbers for illustrations are in boldface.

Notes

Quotes in this book come from an interview by the author with Wynton Marsalis; from his book *Sweet Swing Blues on the Road*; from the video *Marsalis on Music*; or are constructed by the author based on information about Mr. Marsalis from his book and other reference materials.

Page 9, "Participate and you'll understand the fun of being serious": direct quote from *Marsalis on Music*.

Page 10, conversation with Johnny, constructed from two incidents in *Sweet Swing Blues on the Road*.

Page 17, conversation with his mother, constructed from information in reference materials and in *Sweet Swing Blues on the Road*.

Page 20, description of trumpet players' styles, direct quote from *Sweet Swing Blues on the Road*.

Page 24, conversation about music competition: constructed by author.

Page 28, "I had to figure out how to play jazz myself": interview with Wynton Marsalis.

Page 36, "You get a feeling for them": interview with Wynton Marsalis.

Page 38, "to make sure I haven't been wasting time": direct quote from *Sweet Swing Blues on the Road*.

Page 43, "jazzmen in spirit": direct quote from *Sweet Swing Blues on the Road*.

Page 43, "Enjoy being a kid . . .": interview with Wynton Marsalis.

Photo Credit: Michele Malone

ABOUT THE AUTHOR

Margaret Gay Malone is a writer who loves jazz. She plays the vibraphone for fun and loves having "jam sessions" with her husband, Tom, who plays the drums. They live in Sea Cliff, Long Island, with their daughter, Michele, and pet dog and two cats.

Ms. Malone graduated from St. John's University and has had a career in public relations. She has written two other nonfiction books for children as well as a novel for adults.

To Learn More About Wynton Marsalis and His Music

Videos

Marsalis on Music. Sony Classical Film & Video, 1995. This series of four videotapes features Wynton Marsalis teaching children about classical music and jazz.

Books

Marsalis, Wynton. *Marsalis on Music*. New York: W. W. Norton & Company, 1995. Reading level: middle grades. This book, which comes with an audiotape, is a print version of Wynton Marsalis's video series.

Recordings

Wynton Marsalis. Columbia, 1982. Wynton on trumpet when he was twenty-one years old and Branford on saxophone playing jazz.

Wynton Marsalis: Hot House Flowers. Columbia, 1984. Wynton plays solos of old favorites like "Stardust" as well as songs he composed.

Wynton Marsalis Septet: Blue Interlude. Columbia, 1992. Wynton plays in several jazz styles and explains the music to help the listener.

Wynton Marsalis: In This House, on This Morning. Columbia, 1994. Wynton plays gospel music.